SESAME STREET PRESENTS
FOLLOW THAT BIRD!
A Children's Television Workshop Production
The Storybook Based on the Movie

screenplay by
TONY GEISS and JUDY FREUDBERG

**STARRING CAROLL SPINNEY
AS BIG BIRD AND OSCAR THE GROUCH**

and Jim Henson's Sesame Street Muppet performers
and the Sesame Street cast:

Jim Henson
Frank Oz
Richard Hunt
Katherine Mullen
Jerry Nelson
Linda Bove
Emilio Delgado
Loretta Long
Sonia Manzano
Bob McGrath
Roscoe Orman
Alaina Reed
Patricia Leeper
Gordon Robertson
Martin P. Robinson
Cheryl Wagner
Jeff Weiser
Shari Weiser
Bryant Young

also starring:

John Candy
Joe Flaherty
Dave Thomas

with special appearances by:

Benjamin Barret
Liston Bates
Candice Bernstein
Jason Burke
Alyson Court
Adrian McCaulet
Tawny Richard

still photography by Michael Courtney

Executive Producer: Joan Ganz Cooney

Produced by Tony Garnett

Directed by Ken Kwapis

Distributed by Warner Bros.

SESAME STREET PRESENTS

Follow That BIRD!

The Storybook Based on the Movie

adapted by Deborah Hautzig
from the screenplay by Tony Geiss and Judy Freudberg

FEATURING JIM HENSON'S SESAME STREET MUPPETS

Random House / Children's Television Workshop

Weekly Reader Children's Book Club Edition

Copyright © 1985 Warner Bros. Pictures. Sesame Street MUPPETS © Muppets, Inc. 1985. All rights reserved under International and Pan-American Copyright Conventions. ® Sesame Street and the Sesame Street sign are trademarks and service marks of the Children's Television Workshop. Published in the United States by Random House, Inc., New York, and simultaneously in Canada by Random House of Canada Limited. Toronto, in conjunction with the Children's Television Workshop.

Library of Congress Cataloging in Publication Data: Hautzig, Deborah. Sesame Street presents Follow that bird! SUMMARY: Big Bird goes to stay with the Dodo family in Illinois, but soon realizes he really belongs with the variety of inhabitants on Sesame Street. 1. Children's stories, American. [1. Dodo—Fiction. 2. Birds—Fiction. 3. Puppets—Fiction] I. Follow that bird! (Motion picture) II. Title. III. Title: Follow that bird! PZ7.H2888Sf 1985 [E] 84-43052 ISBN: 0-394-87225-8 (trade); 0-394-97225-2 (lib. bdg.)

Last photo in book by Gary Miller.   Manufactured in the United States of America 1 2 3 4 5 6 7 8 9 0

This book is a presentation of **Weekly Reader Children's Book Club.** Weekly Reader Children's Book Club offers book clubs for children from preschool through junior high school. For further information, write to: Weekly Reader Children's Book Club 4343 Equity Drive, Columbus, Ohio 43228.

Weekly Reader Books offers several exciting card and activity programs.
For information, write to WEEKLY READER BOOKS, P.O. Box 16636, Columbus, Ohio 43216.

Big Bird did not know it, but he was in for the adventure of his life! It all began at a meeting of the Feathered Friends Society.

"This meeting will come to order!" said the chairbird. "As you know, our job is to place stray birds with nice bird families." She held up a big picture of Big Bird. "This bird is six years old. He lives all alone with no other birds around."

"Oh, he looks so sad," said an ancient bird.

Mr. Owl said, "That's funny, he looks happy to me."

Miss Finch spoke up. "Nonsense! He can't be happy. He needs to be with a bird family. And I know just the family. . . ."

Big Bird was skating down Sesame Street saying hello to his friends when Miss Finch arrived to find him.

Finally she found him and told him the good news. "You know, Big, you really do need a home," she said.

"But this is my home. I like it here!" said Big Bird.

"But wouldn't you like to be with birds of your own kind?" said Miss Finch. "Wouldn't you be happier in a big birdhouse with a bird family, singing and playing bird games all day long . . . wouldn't you really?"

As Big Bird listened, his eyelids drooped dreamily. He imagined a big happy bird family, and all of them looked just like him. "Gee . . . it sounds wonderful," said Big Bird.

"The Dodo family of Ocean View, Illinois, is waiting to adopt a bird just like you!" said Miss Finch.

"Wow!" said Big Bird. "When can I leave?"

Meanwhile, outside Big Bird's front door, Susan, Maria, and Telly Monster were eavesdropping. "Big Bird is leaving Sesame Street!" Maria said with a gasp. They ran to spread the awful news.

In no time Big Bird was packed and ready to go.

He went to say good-bye to his best friend, Mr. Snuffle-upagus. Both of them burst into tears.

"You can visit me in Ocean View," Big Bird told him.

"I can?" said Snuffy. "That makes me feel a little better."

"Snuffy, please do me a favor. Watch my nest while I'm away, so nothing happens to it, okay?"

"Anything for you, Bird," said Snuffy.

Everyone on Sesame Street came to say good-bye to Big Bird. His beak began to quiver. Saying good-bye was so hard!

"Come on, Big," said Miss Finch. "You don't want to miss your plane! Just walk away and don't look back."

Miss Finch took Big Bird to the airport. He got on the plane with his teddy bear, Radar. Big Bird looked out the window as the plane took off. "Gee, flying is wonderful . . . I feel just like a bird!" he said.

Big Bird fell asleep and didn't wake up until the plane began to land. He looked out at the farms below. "This sure doesn't look like Sesame Street," he said.

When the plane landed in Ocean View, Big Bird was the first one off. He saw the Dodo family right away—Daddy Dodo, Mommy Dodo, and the little Dodos, Donnie and Marie.

Daddy Dodo walked over to Big Bird and said, "Excuse me, was there a big yellow bird on this plane?"

"Only me," said Big Bird.

"Too bad," said Mommy Dodo. "Maybe he'll be on the next plane."

Big Bird looked puzzled. "Are you the Dodos?" he asked. They all nodded. "I'm Big Bird!"

"No, you're not," said Daddy Dodo. "From now on you're Big Dodo!"

"Big Dodo?" said Big Bird, looking more puzzled than ever.

The Dodos lived a short drive from the airport on Canary Row. From the moment Big Bird arrived at their suburban birdhouse, he found life with the Dodos to be puzzling all around.

Every morning, after a big breakfast of birdseed, Daddy Dodo would call out, "Time to go digging for worms!" Then they would all rush out to the front yard and peck and peck and peck . . . but they never found a worm.

Every afternoon Donnie and Marie went swimming in their pool. They were always careful to wear their life preservers . . . even though their pool had only an inch of water.

Every evening the Dodos tried to mow their lawn. They had a lawn mower that they could ride, but they always forgot to get on it. So they ran around in circles chasing it . . . or being chased by it.

One night Daddy Dodo was reading *Newsbeak* magazine and Mommy Dodo was knitting socks with feet at both ends. Big Bird was bored. He decided to try to play with Donnie and Marie.

"Let's play make-believe!" he said. "I'll be Snow White—"

Donnie said, "You're not snow white."

Marie said, "You're bright yellow."

Big Bird continued anyway. "You can be the dwarfs."

"We're not dwarfs," said Donnie.

"We're birds!" said Marie.

Big Bird threw his hands up. "I said *make-believe. Pretend. Imagine!*"

"Okay," said Donnie. "I'll make believe I'm Donnie."

"I'll make believe I'm Marie," said Marie.

"This is fun!" they both said.

Big Bird shook his head sadly.

Big Bird went to his room to write a letter to his friends on Sesame Street. He wanted to tell them that he missed them.

Just then he heard a loud knock on the front door and someone called, "Postcard for Big Bird!"

Big Bird jumped up, banging his head on the ceiling. He rubbed his head and ran downstairs to the door.

The mail carrier handed him a giant postcard. "I hope you don't get any packages from this guy," he said.

Big Bird read the postcard out loud: "'Dear Bird, I am ready to come and visit. Your best friend, Mister Snuffle-upagus.'"

Mommy Dodo said, "What kind of bird is he?"

"He's not a bird," said Big Bird. "He's a snuffle-upagus."

"But your best friend should be a bird," said Daddy Dodo.

"Why?" asked Big Bird.

"Because you're a bird!" said Mommy Dodo. "Soon you'll have a new best friend."

"But I don't want a new best friend. I *have* a best friend. And I want him to come visit!" said Big Bird.

"Oh, you'll get over that," said Daddy Dodo. He stood up. "Come on, everyone, let's dig worms!"

"I don't want to dig worms!" cried Big Bird. "I want to go home!"

All the Dodos giggled. "You *are* home!" they said.

Suddenly Big Bird realized the truth—he was supposed to stay with the Dodos *forever*!

That night Big Bird was so homesick, he could not sleep at all. Finally he made up his mind: He just had to get back to Sesame Street!

So as soon as the sun came up, Big Bird left a note for the Dodos, took Radar, and snuck out the door. "'Bye, Dodos," he whispered. "Thanks for everything.

"It only took two hours to fly here," he told Radar. "We could walk back to Sesame Street in three hours, easy." And off they went.

That evening, back on Sesame Street, Bob was cleaning up Hooper's Store. The evening news was on TV.

"...and now for our final story," the newscaster said, "a runaway with a difference. This runaway is an eight-foot yellow bird."

Bob whirled to look at the TV set. Sure enough, there was a picture of Big Bird. Bob ran to the window.

"Hey, everyone! Come here! Big Bird's run away! It's on TV!"

The Count in his castle saw the news story on his TV set too.

The TV newscaster continued, "With further details, here is our Sesame Street correspondent, Kermit the Frog."

"Hi, ho, Kermit the Frog here, in Ocean View, Illinois, with the thank-you note that Big Bird left saying he was running back to Sesame Street. And here is the family he left, the Dodos."

"Are we on television?" asked Daddy Dodo.

"Uh, yes," said Kermit.

"Goody!" said Mommy Dodo. "Let's go in and watch!"

All the Dodos ran giggling into the house.

"Hey, wait!" said Kermit. "Your interview isn't over."

"Oh, well," sighed Kermit, "so much for the Dodos. Now let's hear from Miss Finch of the Feathered Friends Society. Miss Finch, you sent Big Bird to the Dodos. What are you going to do now?"

"I will find Big Bird," Miss Finch declared. "And I will bring him back to the Dodos where he belongs."

And with that she drove off in her van, leaving Kermit in a cloud of dust.

Meanwhile, far away from Ocean View, Big Bird was watching the whole newscast in a TV store window.

"Oh, no!" he said, looking around nervously. "Radar, we'd better split up."

He put a tag around Radar's neck and marked it "Bear Mail."

"This will throw them off the track," said Big Bird. He kissed Radar and dropped him into a mailbox. "See you on Sesame Street, Radar."

On Sesame Street things were moving fast. Everyone gathered in Hooper's Store to figure out a way to save Big Bird. Bob had a big map.

"We have to find Big Bird before Miss Finch does," said Bob. "There are three roads Big Bird might be on. All three roads meet in a town called Toadstool. This is the plan: We split up into three groups. If none of us finds Big Bird first, we'll meet him in Toadstool."

"Yay!" yelled Oscar. "I love wild-goose chases. Let's go get lost!"

The Sesame Street gang was ready to go!

The Sloppy Jalopy was first, followed by the Volkswagen and the Countmobile.

Ernie and Bert were going by plane.

"Ernie, are you sure you know how to fly this?" asked Bert.

"Trust me," said Ernie as the plane took a nosedive.

Grover was flying too. "This is a job for Super Grover!" he cried.

And far away from Sesame Street and Ocean View—after an uncomfortable night sleeping in a cornfield—Big Bird was walking . . . and walking . . . and walking.

"Sesame Street is a lot farther than I thought," he said. Just then he heard children's voices coming from a farmhouse near the road. "Kids!" he said. And he ran to find them.

A boy and a girl were at the water pump. They were amazed to see Big Bird. "He's the bird we heard about on the evening news, the one that ran away!" said the boy.

"I didn't run away," said Big Bird. "I'm going to my *real* home on Sesame Street." Then he told them about the Dodos and Miss Finch and how hungry he was.

"We'll help you," said the girl. "I'm Ruthie and this is my brother, Floyd." She gave Big Bird a big bowl of birdseed. Big Bird thanked them and hungrily ate it up. Then he helped Ruthie and Floyd feed their chickens.

Big Bird had never been on a farm before. It was so different from the city. Instead of cars honking, there were geese. And there were more animals than people!

Big Bird liked helping the children with their chores. After they fed the chickens, they brought fresh hay to the barn for the horses and cows.

Then they went to the orchard to pick pears. The children needed a ladder but Big Bird did not!

On the way back from the orchard Big Bird caught sight of a familiar red van coming down the road. "Miss Finch!" he whispered. He was in a panic. "What do I do?"

"Quick! Hide! In the hayfield," said Ruthie, pointing across the road.

Big Bird was off like a shot.

In a moment the red van had stopped and Miss Finch stuck her head out the window. "Have you seen an eight-foot yellow bird?" she asked the children.

"No-o-o," they said innocently.

But Miss Finch was not looking at them. She was looking at a yellow feather on the road.

She quickly got out of her van and stomped across the road into the hayfield. "I'll find that bird if it's the last thing I do!" she said.

Suddenly there was a rustle behind her. She whirled around. "Did that haystack move?" she said. She stared at it for a moment. "Impossible," she mumbled, and walked away.

In the distance a haystack with striped legs stood up and ran as fast as it could.

Meanwhile, the Sesame Street gang was getting closer to Toadstool. The Count was zooming along and counting. Ernie and Bert were flying—sometimes upside down.

The yellow VW—minus the fender that Cookie Monster ate—was chugging along. Even the Sloppy Jalopy, after several of Oscar's wild-goose chases, was finally on the right track.

"Birdie, here I come!" yelled Super Grover. But the yellow spot far below was not Big Bird. It was the VW. Grover crashed through the roof!

Big Bird was getting closer to Toadstool too. At last he saw a big sign: "Welcome to Toadstool, the Mushroom City. Today!! The Annual Tournament of Mushrooms Parade!"

Big Bird loved parades. He hurried to the center of Toadstool. He got there just in time to see the parade start—and just in time to see Miss Finch park her van!

"Oh, no! Where will I hide now?" thought Big Bird. He tried to look small but that was impossible. So he started to run and ran right into the middle of the Toadstool Marching Band. Miss Finch ran after him.

When the band turned down one street, Big Bird turned down the other and ran as fast as he could.

Just then the entire Sesame Street gang arrived in Toadstool.

"Look! It's Big Bird!" yelled Maria from the Sloppy Jalopy.

But Big Bird did not hear or see Maria. He was too busy running from Miss Finch.

Big Bird disappeared down a side street and headed out of town. Just outside of Toadstool, he saw a big sign that said "Sleaze Brothers Funfair."

"A carnival! Maybe I can hide here," said Big Bird.

The owners of the carnival noticed the big yellow bird reading their sign. "Look!" said Sid Sleaze to his brother, Sam. "It's the eight-foot runaway bird. We gotta catch him!"

"Yeah," said Sam. "People will pay millions to see that bird."

They strolled over to Big Bird. "You look worried. Maybe we can help you. We own this funfair."

"I'm being chased," said Big Bird breathlessly. "Can I hide in your fair?"

Sam and Sid smiled wickedly. "Be our guest," said Sam. "We have just the place—our hiding cage. You'll be safe there."

They led Big Bird to their Invisible Gorilla cage and Big Bird went in. Then they slammed the door and locked it.

"They'll never find you here," Sam told Big Bird.

"Thanks," said Big Bird.

The two men left and did not come back for several hours.

"Can I come out now?" asked Big Bird when they returned.

Sam laughed. "Don't you like your new cage?"

"*My cage?*" cried Big Bird. "Let me out! Help! Help!"

Sid turned to Sam. "Listen, everyone's looking for a yellow bird. We have to disguise him. And I have just the idea...."

Later that evening, when the crowds began to arrive, Sam stood by the tent selling tickets to see the Bluebird of Happiness. "Eight feet of feathered fun!" Mobs of people poured into the tent.

And there, inside, was Big Bird—dyed bright blue, and singing a very sad song, "No Wonder I'm Blue."

After the show, two children peeked through the curtain.
"Are you real?" said the girl to Big Bird.
A big tear rolled down Big Bird's beak.
"He must be real," said the boy. "He's crying. What's the matter, Bluebird?"
"I'm in big trouble," whispered Big Bird. "Please, would you do me a favor? Call Hooper's Store on Sesame Street and tell my friends where I am!"
Then Sam's head appeared at the tent flap. "Hey, kids! Keep away from the talent."

The children ran outside and found a roadside telephone. "Hello, operator?" said the girl. "Can you tell me how to get to Sesame Street?"

Rrring! A phone rang on Sesame Street...the message got through!

Later that night another call came to Sesame Street, from the Sesame Street rescuers.

"*What?*" said Maria. "Big Bird in a *cage*? He's *blue*? At a *carnival*? ...The Sleaze Brothers! ... Just outside Toadstool. We'll be right there!"

Big Bird was asleep in his cage on the back of the Sleaze Brothers truck. The Sleaze brothers were asleep nearby— clutching piles of dollar bills and smiling.

Suddenly and silently the Sesame Street gang appeared in the tent. They were shocked at what they saw.

"One blue Big Bird locked in a cage!" cried the Count.

They all crept toward the cage. Maria gently woke Big Bird and put her finger to her lips. "Shhh," she said. "We've come to rescue you. Be very quiet."

"This is a job for Super Grover," whispered Grover. He tried to bend apart the bars of the cage, but they would not budge.

"Do you know where the key is?" Linda asked Big Bird in sign language. He pointed toward the sleeping Sleaze brothers.

Linda crept over to snoring Sam. She reached for the keys that were dangling from his hand, but he pulled them back in his sleep. Linda plucked a dollar bill from the pile on his bed and lightly tickled Sam's nose with it. He sneezed and opened his hand. Linda grabbed the keys, but before she could unlock the cage, Sam woke up.

"Hey! The bird!" he yelled. "Let's get out of here!"

Big Bird couldn't wait to tell everyone back home about his exciting rescue and how the Sleaze brothers were arrested for birdnapping.

When they finally got back to Sesame Street, Susan rushed up to Big Bird and gave him a big hug. She also gave him Radar, who had arrived safe and sound in the mail. Everybody was waving and cheering and Big Bird waved back joyfully—until he saw, right there in the crowd, Miss Finch!

She made her way through the crowd. "Hello, Big," she said. "I'm sorry the Dodos weren't right for you. But I can find another bird family."

"He has a family, right here on Sesame Street," Maria told Miss Finch.

"But he would be happier with his own kind!" said Miss Finch.

The Sleaze brothers were out of their beds and into their truck in a flash. Linda had just turned the right key in the lock when the truck roared off, taking with it Big Bird in his cage on the back!

"Help!" yelled Big Bird, clutching the bars.

"Don't worry, Big Bird," Gordon shouted. "We'll rescue you!" Then he and Olivia jumped into the VW.

The chase was on! Olivia pressed the gas pedal all the way to the floor. She had never driven so fast in her life. The beat-up VW began to shake, but slowly it caught up to the Sleaze Brothers truck. Finally it was right behind the truck.

Gordon climbed out and carefully crawled over the front of the VW. He yelled to Big Bird, "Jump! I'll catch you!"

"Gordon, I'm not allowed to jump from a moving truck!" Big Bird yelled back.

"You have my permission!" Gordon said. "Now *jump!*"

And Big Bird did. He jumped right onto the VW and into Gordon's arms.

"We're happy here and we have every kind!" said Maria. "We've got people, monsters, birds, honkers, cows, horses, grouches, frogs . . .".

Miss Finch looked around. She was quite impressed. "Well, he does seem to have a lot of friends who care about him." And then she said, "I've done it again: placed another stray bird in a good home. All right, Big, Sesame Street *is* your home."

Big Bird looked around at all his friends and said, "You bet it is!" Then he remembered that Mr. Snuffle-upagus had promised to watch his nest. "Oh, excuse me, everybody. I have to tell Snuffy I'm back!" And he ran to his nest.

"Snuffy!" said Big Bird.
"Bird!" said Mr. Snuffle-upagus.
The two friends hugged each other.
"I'm glad you're back, Bird," said Mr. Snuffle-upagus.
Big Bird said, "It's so good to be home!"